Samantha the Swimming Fairy

For all the children of
Newbridge Primary School

Special thanks to
Sue Mongredien

ISBN 978-0-545-20256-5

All rights reserved. Published by Scholastic Inc., 557 Broadway, New York, NY 10012, by arrangement with Rainbow Magic Limited.

SCHOLASTIC, LITTLE APPLE, and associated logos are trademarks and/or registered trademarks of Scholastic Inc. RAINBOW MAGIC is a trademark of Rainbow Magic Limited. Reg. U.S. Patent & Trademark Office and other countries. HIT and the HIT logo are trademarks of HIT Entertainment Limited.

12 11 10 9 8 7 6 5 4 3 2   10 11 12 13 14 15/0

Printed in the U.S.A.   40

First Scholastic Printing, April 2010

Samantha
the Swimming
Fairy

by Daisy Meadows

SCHOLASTIC INC.

New York   Toronto   London   Auckland
Sydney   Mexico City   New Delhi   Hong Kong

The
Fairyland
Palace

Fairyla

Parking Lot

Buses

Cooke Soccer
Stadium

Riding Stables

Basketball Courts

Soccer
Fields

Tippington
Town

REC CENTER

Swimming Pool

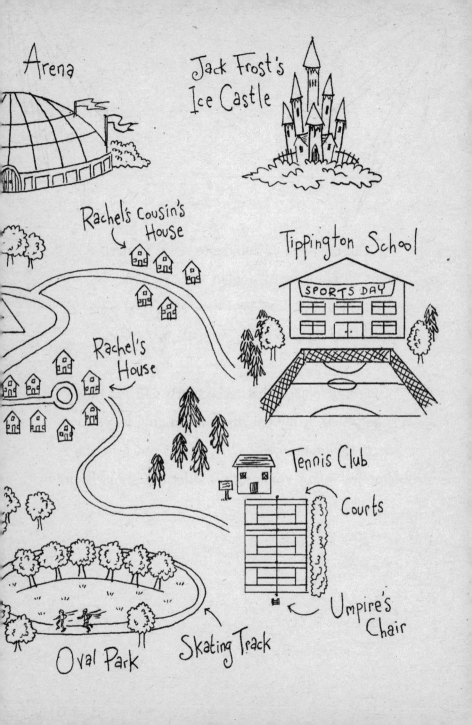

The Fairyland Olympics are about to start,
And my crafty goblins will take part.
We'll win this year, for I have a cunning plan.
I'll send my goblins to compete in Fairyland.

The magic objects that make sports safe and fun
Will be stolen by my goblins, to keep until we've won.
Sports Fairies, prepare to lose and to watch us win.
Goblins, follow my commands, and let the games begin!

Contents

Swimming Pool Puzzle

"Fetch, Buttons!" Rachel Walker called, throwing her dog's favorite ball across the yard.

Kirsty Tate, Rachel's best friend, was staying with the Walkers for spring break. She smiled. "Buttons loves exercise, doesn't he?" she said, as the dog bounded after the ball. "And we're almost as fit as

he is. We've had such an athletic week!"

Rachel grinned. Without her parents knowing, Rachel and Kirsty had been taking part in a new fairy adventure this week. They were helping the Sports Fairies track down their missing magic objects. Rachel thought that she and Kirsty were the luckiest girls in the world since they were friends with the fairies.

"Good dog!" said Rachel's dad, coming out to the yard with Mrs. Walker. Buttons rushed back with the ball in his mouth, then dropped it at Rachel's feet and went to his water bowl for a drink.

"Phew, it's hot," Mrs. Walker said, fanning herself. "It's the perfect day for a swim."

Rachel and Kirsty looked at each other excitedly. Swimming would be a great idea—especially since Samantha the Swimming Fairy's magic goggles were still missing.

"Oh, yes, can we go swimming?" Rachel asked.

"The Tippington pool is closed," Mr.

Walker pointed out, "so you'd have to go
to Aqua World in the next town over."
Then he frowned. "But I took the car into
the garage to be fixed, so I won't be able
to drive you there."

Kirsty felt disappointed. She loved
swimming! At the beginning of the week,
she and Rachel had discovered that Jack
Frost's mischievous goblins had stolen the
Sports Fairies' magic objects. When the
objects were with the Sports Fairies — or
in their lockers in the Fairyland Arena —
the objects made sure that sports in the
human world and in Fairyland were
safe, fun, and fair. But, when they
weren't in place, only the people who
were very close to a magic object were
good at that particular sport. Sports

everywhere were being ruined!

The Fairyland Olympics were starting soon, and Jack Frost wanted his goblins to use the objects' powers to win the big prize—a golden cup full of luck. Kirsty and Rachel knew that the goblins were practicing hard for their events, so the goblins with Samantha's magic goggles must be in a swimming pool somewhere.

"You could take the bus to Aqua World," Mrs. Walker said. "The 41 goes all the way there. If you take your cell phone, Rachel, you can let me know when you'll be back."

"Hooray!" cheered Rachel and Kirsty together. They both rushed inside to pack their swimming things. Then Rachel's mom walked them to the bus stop.

They didn't have to wait long before
a bus pulled up. The girls waved good-
bye to Mrs. Walker and sat together at
the back of the bus where the seats were
slightly higher, so they
could easily see out
the window. Kirsty
gazed out at the
houses, and the bus
started up.

As they waited at
a traffic light, Kirsty noticed that they
had stopped near the Tippington
swimming pool. A sign outside read
CLOSED FOR MAINTENANCE. The building
had a glass front. It was tinted at the
bottom to keep people from looking
in, but it was clear at the top. A huge

pipe wrapped around the outside of the building. Kirsty guessed it must be a water slide.

Suddenly, Kirsty noticed something green flash above the tinted glass. She blinked and stared. What was it?

The green thing appeared again, and Kirsty let out a gasp. She was sure she'd just seen a goblin!

Goblins Galore!

Kirsty nudged Rachel. "Look!" she cried, pointing.

As the girls watched, the goblin popped up again and Rachel's eyes sparkled with excitement. "I can't believe you spotted him!" she exclaimed. "How lucky is that? If he's in there, I bet Samantha's magic goggles are, too."

"But why does he keep popping up and

then disappearing?" Kirsty wondered, as the goblin bounced above the tinted glass once more.

"He must be jumping on the diving board." Rachel giggled. She stood up and pressed the button to tell the bus driver that they wanted to get off. "Come on," she said, "let's investigate. We can go to Aqua World later."

Kirsty jumped up eagerly. Another fairy adventure was beginning!

At the bus stop, the girls got off and hurried back toward the pool.

"I didn't notice the goblin wearing any goggles," Kirsty said.

"I didn't either," Rachel agreed. "But maybe there are two of them in there."

Kirsty and Rachel went around to the side of the building and pressed their faces up against the glass so that they could see in more clearly. They both gasped in amazement.

"There are goblins everywhere!" Rachel cried.

The whole pool was full of green goblins of all sizes. Some were diving, others were swimming laps, and some were just playing in the shallow end.

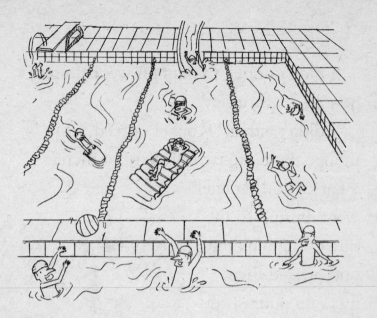

"We'd better get in there and start looking for the magic goggles," Kirsty said. "It might take us a while."

The girls snuck around the building, looking for a way inside. Unfortunately, the whole place seemed locked. Then Rachel heard footsteps, and the girls hid behind a bush. They peeked through the leaves, and saw someone coming toward them.

It was a goblin, wrapped in a big, striped beach towel. He was wearing a white swim cap and red goggles on his head!

"Are those Samantha's magic goggles?" Rachel asked Kirsty in a whisper.

Kirsty shook her head. "I think those are just ordinary ones," she whispered back. "They don't look magical. The other magic objects have all sparkled with fairy magic."

The girls watched as the goblin walked to a nearby tree and climbed up into its branches. He started crawling along a thick branch that led to an open window

in the building. The goblin reached the
window and pulled himself through it.
Then he disappeared from view.

"So that's how they've been getting in,"
Kirsty said. "Let's try it."

Kristy and Rachel climbed up the tree,
along the branch, and in through the
window, just like the goblin had done. The
girls found themselves in a hallway with
tiles on the floor and walls.

"I know where we are," Rachel said.
"The pools are this way."

She led Kirsty down
the hallway. Faint
shouts and squeals of
excitement echoed
up from the pools.
The the girls tiptoed
along, not wanting to
be seen.

At the end of the
hallway, they peeked
around the corner.
Kirsty saw two pools,
a large one with a
water slide at the far
end, and a smaller, more shallow pool
in front. In the small pool, seven goblins,
all wearing nose plugs, floated on the

surface. They were on their backs with
their heads together in the middle of the
pool. Their legs were pointing out to the
sides. It reminded Kirsty of a wheel, with
the goblins as the spokes. "What are they
doing?" she murmured.

Rachel tried not to laugh out loud.
"They're practicing synchronized

swimming!" she whispered. "I don't see
any sparkles around their goggles though,
do you?"

The girls stared carefully at the goggles
on the goblins' heads, but they all looked
pretty ordinary.

Then the goblins flipped over into
handstands, with their bodies underwater

and their legs sticking out, toes pointed.
They all lowered their left legs, and
turned in the water at the same time.

"Come on, let's sneak by while they're
underwater," Kirsty said. "Then we can
search the main pool."

The girls raced past the small pool, and
hid behind a pile of floats. Then Rachel
noticed something
interesting. She
nudged Kirsty. "Do
you see those floats
over there?" she
asked, pointing to a
stack at the water's
edge. "They're
shimmering with pink sparkles!"

"Maybe the magic goggles are over

there," Kirsty whispered. "Let's go and check."

The two friends ran over for a closer look. There was no sign of the magic goggles, but both girls smiled when they saw what was making the sparkles. Perched on top of the pile of floats, with her tiny legs dangling over the edge, was Samantha the Swimming Fairy!

Goggle Guard

Samantha had long, dark hair, and
a pink-and-black swimsuit with a pretty
pink sarong-style skirt. "Hello there,
girls!" she said cheerfully.

"Hello." Rachel smiled. "We were just
searching for your magic goggles!"

"Me, too," Samantha said. "I can
sense that they're in this building." She

grinned at the girls. "But I can't let you stay in those jeans and T-shirts! I'll get you something more appropriate . . ." She waved her wand and a stream of glittering, powder-pink fairy dust swirled from its tip and whirled around the girls. Seconds later, their clothes were replaced with two-piece swimsuits with ruffled skirts on the bottoms. Rachel's was lilac with a silvery dolphin pattern, and Kirsty's was turquoise with a gold seashell print.

"That's more like it!" Samantha smiled.

"Oh, thank you," Kirsty said, admiring her suit. "Now we should try looking in the big pool for your goggles, Samantha. None of the goblins in the little pool have them."

Rachel pointed to the bleacher seats that ran along the side of the main pool. "Let's duck behind those," she suggested. "Then we can peek out to look for the goggles and stay hidden."

"Good idea," Samantha agreed.

Together, the two girls and their fairy friend snuck behind the plastic seating, and peeked out between the chairs.

Kirsty noticed a goblin wearing a T-shirt that said LIFEGUARD on the front.

He was sitting in an extra tall chair by the side of the pool. He kept shouting instructions to the other goblins. But Kirsty's eye was caught by what dangled from his left hand—a pair of sparkling pink goggles! "Over there," she whispered to her friends. "I think he has the magic goggles!"

Samantha beamed. "Yes, those *are* my goggles!" she cheered quietly. "Nice find!"

"Now we just need to think of a way to get a hold of them," Rachel said thoughtfully.

"How about I turn you both into fairies?" Samantha suggested. "That way we can try to fly really close to the lifeguard without him noticing—and, with a little luck, we can sneak the goggles right out of his hand."

Rachel and Kirsty nodded.

"Yes, let's try it," Kirsty said eagerly.

Samantha waved her wand, and a cloud of light pink sparkles spun around the girls again. This time, they felt themselves shrinking down, down, down until they were fairy-size.

It's always so exciting to turn into a fairy! thought Kirsty. She fluttered her wings happily, loving the way they glittered with all the colors of the rainbow under the bright lights above the pool.

"Let's go grab some goggles." Rachel giggled as she zoomed into the air. Kirsty and Samantha followed, keeping as close to the ceiling as they could so that the goblins in the pool wouldn't notice them.

As they got closer to the lifeguard, Rachel could hear him bragging.

"I'm the lifeguard, so that means I'm in charge," he was telling some other goblins. "And I say no splashing, no cannonballs, and no dunking!"

"We're just having a little fun," a small goblin replied. "You're a bully!"

"Rules are rules!" answered the lifeguard. He pointed to his T-shirt in a self-important manner. "Read the shirt!" he ordered. "I'm the lifeguard—what I say goes!"

Kirsty, Rachel, and Samantha hovered behind the lifeguard's chair, waiting for a good moment to grab the goggles. But the lifeguard kept a tight grip on them. Then he would twirl them around his finger from time to time.

Now a different goblin with a mischievous expression approached. "It's my turn to have those," he said, pointing to the magic goggles. "You've had them for days, and you're not even using them! I want to wear them on the water slide."

"No way," the lifeguard huffed. "Water-sliding is not an Olympic sport! Remember, we came here to practice Olympic water events, not to play around on slides."

"But—" the other goblin began, yet there was no stopping the lifeguard.

"Have you forgotten that the Fairyland Olympics are only two days away?" he continued. "Two days! That's all you've got! You should be practicing your strokes instead of going on the slide. Jack Frost won't be very happy if he hears about this."

The other goblin stomped off with a grumpy look on his face. Kirsty thought the lifeguard goblin looked kind of smug as he watched him go. He twirled the magic goggles around his finger again.

The three fairies exchanged glances and flew a little closer. They hoped they could slip the goggles off the lifeguard's finger and fly away with them. But just then, a cry of alarm came from the water.

"Help!"

Kirsty, Rachel, and Samantha all turned to see what was happening. A goblin was flailing around in the deep end of the pool. He was thrashing his arms and splashing water everywhere.

"Help!" he sputtered again. Then, before the girls knew what was happening, he slipped under the water.

A Tricky Thief

The lifeguard immediately put the
magic goggles on and dived into
the water with a huge splash.

The three fairies watched as he
swam across the pool, his long green
arms scooping through the water in
a perfect freestyle. In just a few strong
strokes, he'd reached the struggling
goblin and was pulling him to safety.

He popped the magic goggles on top of
his head as he reached the side of the
pool.

"Wow!" Rachel said admiringly. "He's
an amazing swimmer—or, I guess I
should say your goggles are amazing,
Samantha, for helping him swim so well."

Samantha nodded. "They are very
powerful goggles," she agreed with pride.
Then her eyes widened. "What's going
on over there?"

Kirsty and Rachel looked and saw
that the goblin who'd asked to borrow
the magic goggles was now swimming
up behind the lifeguard goblin. Suddenly,

he reached out his
arm and grabbed
the magic goggles
from the top of the
lifeguard's head.
Then he swam off
with them, heading
toward the water
slide.

"That was *so* tricky!"
Rachel exclaimed.

"The lifeguard didn't notice a thing,"
Kirsty added, watching as the lifeguard
pulled the struggling goblin out of the
water and onto the deck of the pool.

The rescued goblin sputtered and coughed. "I thought I was going blind!" he wailed.

"Blind? Why?" the lifeguard asked.

The rescued goblin coughed again. "I got water in my eyes and it stung," he explained.

"Ahh," the lifeguard said, wagging a finger. "If you want to keep water out of your eyes, you need a pair of goggles like mine."

The rescued goblin frowned. "But you're not wearing any goggles," he replied, sounding confused.

The lifeguard clicked his tongue in an impatient way. "Well, I keep them up here when I'm not actually swimming," he explained, pointing a finger at the top of his head, where the magic goggles had been just seconds earlier.

"Up where? I can't see them!" the rescued goblin said, completely confused now.

The lifeguard rolled his eyes. "Then you need glasses, not goggles!" he snapped. "Or maybe a new brain," he muttered. "Honestly!"

Samantha, Kirsty, and Rachel couldn't help laughing.

"Come on, that rescued goblin's fine.
Let's find the tricky goblin who took my
goggles," Samantha said.

The three friends flew across the pool,
looking for the shimmer of the magic
goggles. The water was still full of
goblins, but after a minute or so, Kirsty
caught a glimpse of pink sparkles and
pointed it out to her friends.

"There!" she said. "He's swimming in

the deep end. Can you see him?"

Rachel and Samantha both watched.
The goblin with the goggles was
slicing through the water with a very
strong freestyle.

The three friends flew after the goblin,
but he was going very fast. Before they
had a chance to catch up, he'd reached
the other end of the pool. He was
headed for the entrance to the water

slide. He got out, pushing the goggles
onto his head. Then he climbed up the
steps to the slide, cutting in front of
a whole crowd of goblins who were
waiting their turn. "Let me past! Get out

of the way!" he shouted. "Goblin with
goggles coming through!"

It wasn't long before a shoving match

broke out between the goblins at the top of the slide.

"Stop pushing!" shouted one.

"Wait your turn!" cried another.

"You're stepping on my toes!" whined somebody else.

Kirsty, Rachel, and Samantha looked at one another in despair. What were they going to do now? The magic goggles were surrounded by goblins!

Spotted!

Rachel racked her brain, but it was hard to concentrate because it was so noisy. Two goblins were having an argument in the pool down below.

"It's my turn for the inner tube," said the taller of the goblins, trying to grab it from the other's hands.

"No way! I just got it!" the second

43

goblin snapped. "It won't fit you anyway. It's too small for you."

The tall goblin looked upset and splashed the second goblin in the face before angrily swimming away.

But their fight had given Rachel an idea. "Samantha, would you be able to make an inner tube with your magic?" she asked.

"Of course," said Samantha, holding out her wand.

"And could you make it slightly

smaller than usual, please?" Rachel
went on.

Samantha nodded. "No problem,"
she replied. "Why?"

"Well," Rachel began, "I was thinking
that we could hold it at the bottom of
the water slide. Then, when the goblin
with the magic goggles comes shooting
off of the slide, he'll go straight into the
inner tube. And, if the inner tube's a little
tight, it might trap his arms by his sides."

Kirsty grinned. "And then we'll be able
to take the magic goggles right off his
head!" she finished. "That's pure genius,
Rachel!"

Samantha was smiling. "I love it," she
agreed. "And I can use my fairy magic
to make the ring just the right size to
pin the goblin's arms to his sides without

hurting him. Let's see . . ." She muttered some magical words and waved her wand. Bright pink fairy dust shot from the end of it, and then a tiny turquoise inner tube appeared out of nowhere. It floated in midair.

Rachel beamed. "Perfect," she said, reaching up to take it.

"I made the inner tube extra small for now, so we can carry it easily and the goblins won't be able to see it," Samantha said. "I'll make it bigger when we're ready to use it. Let's go over by the bottom of the slide and wait for our goblin."

The three fairies carried the inner tube through the air and hovered near the end of the water slide. Lots of goblins were swooshing down the slide, one after another, and splashing into the pool.

"There's our goblin," Kirsty said,
spotting him as he scooted onto his belly
at the top of the slide. "But how are we
going to keep track of where he is when
he's in the tube?" she asked. "It's going
to be tricky to catch the right goblin if
we don't know when the goblin with
the goggles is going to pop out of the
tunnel."

Samantha winked
and waved her
wand. A stream
of sparkles shot
through the air
toward the goblin
as he pushed off
into the giant tube.
"There." She
giggled. "I just

made his swimming trunks glow bright
blue. We should be able to see them
shining, even when he's in the tunnel."

Rachel laughed. "There he is!" she
cried, pointing when a bright blue glow
flashed by a window in the tube.

"He's getting closer," Kirsty said,
as they saw the blue glow zip around a
twisty section of pipe and approach the
bottom. "Let's get into position!"

Samantha waved her wand to make the
inner tube bigger. She and the girls were
getting ready to lower it into the right
place, when they heard someone yell from
the other end of the pool.

"Hey, look out! There are pesky fairies
near the slide!"

Kirsty glanced over her shoulder and
gulped. Several angry-looking goblins were
pointing and swimming toward them.

She looked nervously at Rachel and
Samantha. "We won't be able to catch
the goblin on the slide if all the other
goblins come after us," she cried. "What
are we going to do?"

Making Waves

"I'll take care of this," Samantha said, pointing her wand at the water. A rush of bubbles and sparkles streamed from the tip of her wand and into the pool. Immediately, huge waves appeared and began rolling toward the crowd of goblins. It was as if a wave machine had been switched on!

53

At first, the goblins tried to push through the waves and reach the fairies, but then Samantha twirled her wand, and a bunch of surfboards and beach balls appeared.

"Hey, I'm a super-surfer!" one goblin shouted, grabbing a board and riding a wave back to the shallow end. "Woohoo!"

After that, all the goblins wanted to be super-surfers. Some lay on boards and coasted along on the waves, while others tried to jump up

and stand. Soon they were
all whooping with
glee and playing
in the waves. They
had completely
forgotten about
the fairies! Rachel
and Kirsty
couldn't help
but giggle.
"They won't
bother us anymore,"
Samantha said.
"Now let's get the
one with my goggles.
Look, he's just about
to come out of the slide!"
Sure enough, the goblin with
the magic goggles was

coming down the final stretch.

The three fairies gripped the inner
tube tightly.

"Here he comes!" Kirsty cried, and,
a second later, the goblin with the magic
goggles burst headfirst off the slide,
straight into the inner tube!

Thanks to Samantha's magic, the tube
was just the right size to pin his arms
to his sides. When the girls let go, the
goblin was left
bobbing up
and down in
the water like
a big green
cork.

Samantha
flew over and
tugged at the
rubber strap of her magic
goggles. Kirsty and Rachel fluttered over
to help her.

"Hey!" shouted the goblin, scowling.
"Those goggles are mine!"

"Oh, no they're not," Samantha told
him sternly. As the goggles came free,

they shrank to
their Fairyland–
size and
Samantha
dangled them in
front of his face.
"Besides," she
went on with a

clever smile, "I don't think they would
fit you now!"

Samantha touched her wand to the
goggles and they sparkled even more
brightly for a moment. Kirsty and
Rachel knew that now that the magic
goggles were back with Samantha,
their powers would start working again.
Soon, swimming would be fun and safe
in the human world and throughout
Fairyland.

"Hooray!" Rachel cheered happily, as she, Samantha, and Kirsty zoomed safely up and out of the goblin's reach. Then Samantha put on her magic goggles and used her magic to calm the waves and lift the inner tube off the goblin, setting him free. He splashed off miserably to join his friends.

The lifeguard goblin, seeing what had happened, shouted grumpily, "Everyone out of the pool. It's time to go back to Jack Frost's castle."

All the goblins reluctantly climbed out of the pool, collected their towels and clothes, and marched off. It was very quiet once they had left.

"What a mess!" Kirsty said, gazing down at all the floats, tubes, and bodyboards still bobbing around in the water.

"This won't take long to clean up," Samantha promised. She waved her wand again. In a swirl of light pink fairy

dust, the floats and toys rose up out of
the water and put themselves away. The
inner tubes rolled into the cabinet like
big, colorful wheels.

Once the pool was back to normal, the
three friends flew out through the open
window. Then Samantha used her magic
to turn Kirsty and Rachel back into girls
wearing outdoor clothes again.

"I need to go back to Fairyland, to
make sure everything's ready for the
swimming events in the Fairyland
Olympics," Samantha said, kissing
Rachel and Kirsty good-bye. "Thank
you so much for your help. Where
are you going now?"

"We need to catch a bus to Aqua
World," Rachel said.

Samantha nodded and waved her wand

in a complicated pattern. A pink, glittery ticket appeared in each girl's hand. "This'll be quicker," Samantha said. "When you're ready, just touch the tickets together. They're full of special fairy dust, and will take you right to Aqua World."

"Oh, thank you!" Kirsty cried, looking at her ticket in delight. What an exciting day this was turning out to be!

The girls said good-bye to Samantha

and watched as she flew off into the distance.

"That was fun," Rachel said, holding her ticket out toward Kirsty's. "And I'm really looking forward to doing some swimming myself, now."

"Me, too," Kirsty agreed, touching her ticket to Rachel's and feeling herself getting swept up by fairy magic. "But not as much as I'm looking forward to how we get there!"

THE SPORTS FAIRIES

Now Rachel and Kirsty must help

Alice

the Tennis Fairy!

Jack Frost's goblins have stolen
Alice's magic tennis racket. Can Rachel
and Kirsty help track it down?

Join their next adventure
in this special sneak peek!

Goblindon

"Isn't it a beautiful day, Kirsty?" Rachel Walker said happily. She and her best friend, Kirsty Tate, were walking along a country path not far from the Walkers' house, enjoying the sunshine. "And it would be even better if we could find another magic object!"

"Yes!" Kirsty agreed. "The Fairyland Olympics start tomorrow, and Alice the

Tennis Fairy's magic racket and Gemma the Gymnastics Fairy's magic hoop are still missing."

As the girls walked down the lane, Rachel suddenly noticed a strange sign pinned to a tree. "Look at that," she remarked, pointing it out to Kirsty.

The words on the sign were painted in bright green paint and looked very sloppy. "*Goblindon,*" Kirsty read aloud. "And there's an arrow with the words ENTRANCE TO TIPPINGTON TENNIS CLUB written underneath it," she added.

"Oh no!" Rachel exclaimed. "This has got goblin mischief written all over it! Mom and I have played tennis at that club once or twice and there are always lots of people around. What if the goblins have been spotted by someone?"

Kirsty looked worried. The girls knew that nobody in the human world was supposed to find out about Fairyland and the goblins, fairies, and other creatures that lived there.

"We have to find out what's going on," Kirsty insisted. "If the goblins are at the tennis club, they might have Alice's magic racket."

SPECIAL EDITION

Three Books in One!
More Rainbow Magic Fun!

■SCHOLASTIC
www.scholastic.com
www.rainbowmagiconline.com

HiT entertainment

RMSPECIAL2

RAINBOW magic

These activities are magical!

Play dress-up, send friendship notes, and much more!

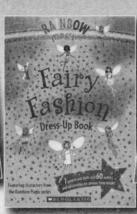

SCHOLASTIC

www.scholastic.com

www.rainbowmagiconline.com

HiT entertainment

RMACTIV2

THE PUPPY PLACE

SO MANY PERFECT PUPPIES – COLLECT THEM ALL!